LEARNING TO RIDE.

The bike moved forward. She was riding!

Not for long.

The bike started to wobble. Posey gripped the handlebars harder, but it shook from side to side.

She forgot how to stop.

She forgot to put her feet down.

She was going so fast . . . she was too afraid!

CRASH!

Read all the books starring
PRINCESS POSEY, FIRST GRADER!

PRINCESS PSEY

and the

CRAZY, LAZY VACATION

Stephanie Greene

ILLUSTRATED BY

Stephanie Roth Sisson

PUFFIN BOOKS

PUFFIN BOOKS
Published by Penguin Random House LLC
375 Hudson Street
New York, New York 10014

Published simultaneously in the United States of America by G. P. Putnam's Sons and
Puffin Books, imprints of Penguin Random House LLC, 2016

THE LIBRARY OF CONGRESS HAS CATALOGED THE G.P. PUTNAM'S SONS EDITION AS FOLLOWS:
Greene, Stephanie.
Princess Posey and the crazy, lazy vacation/Stephanie Greene; illustrated by Stephanie Roth Sisson.
pages cm
Summary: "First-grader Posey is concerned that her spring vacation will be boring compared to
her friends' travels, but her mother's plan to take each day as it comes turns out to be full of
excitement."—Provided by publisher.
ISBN 978-0-399-16963-2 (hardcover)
[1.Family life—Fiction. 2. Vacations—Fiction.]
I. Sisson, Stephanie Roth, illustrator. II. Title.
PZ7.G8434 Pmh 2015
[E]—dc23
2014031152

Puffin Books ISBN 978-0-14-751293-2

Decorative graphics by Marikka Tamura. Design by Marikka Tamura.
Text set in Stempel Garamond.

Printed in the United States of America

1 3 5 7 9 10 8 6 4 2

For Oliver, who loved his leisure time
—S.G.

To my dear friend Dina Young
—S.R.S.

CONTENTS

SPRING VACATION

It was the day before spring vacation. After lunch, everyone helped Miss Lee clean the class-room.

Posey, Nikki, Ava, and Grace worked in the art corner.

Posey put the scissors in the scissors bin. Ava and Nikki sorted

1

the colored paper into piles. Grace's job was to collect the colored markers.

"You know what's impossible?" said Posey.

"What?" said Nikki.

"It's impossible to count all the hairs on your head."

Grace and Ava and Nikki giggled. They loved to play the impossible game. Lots of kids in their grade played it.

"You know what's impossible?" said Nikki. "It's impossible to count all the leaves on a tree."

"My turn," said Grace. "You know what's impossible? It's impossible to talk if you are dead."

"What if you're a ghost?" said Posey.

They giggled again.

Miss Lee came over to them. "You four are being very silly today," she said.

"That's because vacation is tomorrow!" said Posey.

"We're going to be silly for a whole week," Ava said.

"I'm sure you are." Miss Lee

turned to the rest of the class. "We're almost out of time," she called. "Finish what you are doing. Then get whatever you're taking home and line up."

Posey got her things and stood in the car line. Ava, Nikki, and Grace got into the bus line.

"I hope you all have a wonderful vacation and come back to school exhilarated!" Miss Lee said.

That was their new "exciting" word. Miss Lee had started teaching them a new one every week. They learned the meaning and how to spell it.

"That means 'happy'!" a boy shouted.

"Very, *very* happy," said Posey.

"Great job, both of you." Miss Lee smiled. "The Monday we get back, you can write a story about what you did and share it with the class."

Everyone started to talk about their plans.

"We're going to Florida," Luca said.

"I'm going to stay with my *nani* in New York City," said Rashmi.

Posey frowned. She didn't know what they were doing on vacation.

Her mom was taking the week off. But Posey didn't think they were going anywhere.

How could she be exhilarated if all they did was stay home?

THAT DOESN'T SOUND FUN

Her mom was waiting for her in the line of cars. Posey got into the backseat with Danny.

"Are we going anywhere on vacation?" she asked.

"Hello to you, too," said her mom.

"Hi," Posey said. "Are we?"

"Nope."

"Then what are we doing?" Posey buckled her seat belt.

"Nothing." Her mom sounded happy about it.

"That doesn't sound like a very fun vacation," Posey grumbled.

"We'll make it fun," her mom said.

"Can I sleep over at Gramps's house?" Posey asked.

"Gramps is driving Mrs. Romero to visit her sister."

"No fair." Posey slid down in her seat. She crossed her arms over her chest.

Her mom smiled at her in the rearview mirror. "All we do is rush, rush, rush," she said. "We need a nice, lazy vacation."

"What does that mean?" said Posey.

"We won't make any plans," said her mom. "We'll wake up every day and see what we feel like doing."

"That sounds boring."

Her mom laughed. "Wait and see. You might be in for a surprise."

CHAPTER
THREE

THE ZOMBIE

On Saturday, it rained.

"I'm staying in my pajamas all day," Posey said.

"Me, too," said her mom. "We might even have pancakes for dinner."

"For dinner?" Posey shouted.

They ate breakfast on the couch and watched cartoons.

Then Posey played blocks with Danny. He knocked everything down.

"Why's Danny so cranky?" she asked.

"He's getting a new molar tooth," her mom told her. "He was up half the night."

Posey went up to her room. She read her favorite books.

She colored.

She tried different
clips in her hair.

Then she put on
her tutu and made a
castle with the pillows and blanket
from her bed. She put her stuffed
animals inside and crawled in with
them.

She was Princess Posey, the
brave princess who protected
the castle.

After a while, her mom came upstairs. "I'm putting Danny down for a nap," she said. "Keep your fingers crossed."

Danny cried for a long time.

Finally, he fell asleep.

"So far, so good," whispered a voice.

Posey poked her head out of the castle. Her mom was in the doorway. Her face was bright blue. There was a circle around each eye and one around her mouth.

"You look like a blue clown," said Posey.

"Shhhh . . ." Her mom held her finger to her mouth. "It's a clay mask," she whispered.

"You look so funny," Posey whispered back.

"I know. Come help me make cookies."

Posey tiptoed down the stairs behind her mom. Just as they reached the bottom, the doorbell rang.

It was very loud.

Posey's mom yanked the door open before the bell could ring again.

"*Shhhhh!*" she hissed.

The delivery man with a package in his hands froze.

His mouth fell open. His eyebrows flew up.

Posey's mom silently took the package from him. "Thank you," she mouthed.

She smiled her clown smile and shut the door.

Posey put her hand over her mouth and followed her mom to the kitchen. They burst out laughing.

"He must have thought I was crazy," her mom said.

"You look crazy," said Posey.

"The poor man." Her mom slapped her hand to her chest. "I scared him half to death."

"He looked like a zombie." Posey opened her eyes and mouth wide. She raised her arms in slow motion.

That made her mom laugh harder.

For the rest of the day, every time Posey did her zombie imitation, her mom laughed and laughed.

CHAPTER
FOUR

A LOOSE TOOTH

Sunday morning was sunny and warm. The minute Posey woke up, she felt something funny.

"Mom! You won't believe it!" she shouted.

She ran into her mom's bedroom

and jumped on her bed. "I have a loose tooth! Look!"

Her mom sat up. "Let me see."

Posey opened her mouth wide. She wiggled her top tooth with her tongue. "I felt it as soon as I woke up," she said.

"That looks very loose," said her mom.

Posey wiggled her tooth again. It felt so exciting. "Let's eat breakfast outside to celebrate!" she said.

"Great idea."

Posey ran downstairs and opened the back door. Two red cardinals darted off the bird feeder. Robins pecking in the grass flew up into the apple tree.

Next door, Nick and Tyler were riding their bikes in their driveway.

They had used bricks and a board to make a ramp. They rode their bikes up the ramp and jumped off the end.

They practiced every day after school.

Posey ran back inside. "Can I ride my bike today?" she asked.

"You were too big for it at the end of last year, remember?" said her mom.

"I want to try."

"Okay. Let's have breakfast first."

❀ ❀ ❀

The garage was so messy. There was hardly room for their car. Gramps had hung Posey's small bike on hooks for the winter. It had training wheels.

Her mom took it down and put it on the driveway.

Posey sat on it and tried to pedal. Her knees hit the handlebars.

"I was afraid of that," her mom said.

"No fair," said Posey.

When she started to get off, Danny tried to climb on.

"No, Danny, it's mine." Posey sat down again.

"Here, Danny." Their mom wheeled out Danny's plastic truck. He climbed on and pushed it across the driveway with his feet.

"How come Danny gets to ride?" said Posey.

"Seems to me that a girl with a loose tooth needs a bigger bike."

"Really?" Posey jumped up. "Can we buy one?"

"We'll go tomorrow," her mom said.

"Why not today?"

"I need to clean out the garage before we put another thing in it," her mom said.

"Wait till I tell Tyler and Nick!" Posey shouted.

She ran over to the boys. "I'm getting a new bike tomorrow."

"Are you getting those dopey training wheels again?" said Nick.

If Nick called them "dopey," Posey didn't want them. "Of course not," she said.

"Good thing." Nick rode his bike up the ramp. He gave a loud shout when he jumped off the end.

"I have a loose tooth, too. See?" Posey wiggled it back and forth, but the boys didn't look.

Posey didn't mind. Today, she had a loose tooth.

Tomorrow, she would have a new bike.

Soon, she could do stunts, too.

CHAPTER
FIVE

GOING TOO FAST

Posey's new bike was ocean blue. The handlebars had streamers at the end. It had a striped seat.

Her new helmet had stripes, too.

The man at the store made Posey straddle the bike to make sure it was the right size.

"What about training wheels?"
he asked Posey's mom.

"I don't want them," Posey said
quickly.

"You sure?" the man asked.

Posey nodded.

"Okay, well, when you need to

stop, you pedal backward." He showed her. "You can also put your feet on the ground."

He held the bike steady while Posey sat on the seat. She put her feet on the pedals. They felt just right. She pedaled backward. They stopped halfway.

"See? That's all it takes," said the man.

"That's easy," Posey said.

He showed her how to put down the kickstand. Then he said, "It's all yours."

When they got home, her mom lifted the bike out of the trunk.

"Wait until I get the groceries inside," she said. "I'll help you."

Posey was too excited to wait.

She straddled the bike and put one foot on the pedal. She hopped onto the seat and pushed down on the other pedal with her other foot.

The bike moved forward. She was riding!

Not for long.

The bike started to wobble. Posey gripped the handlebars harder, but it shook from side to side.

She forgot how to stop.

She forgot to put her feet down.

She was going so fast . . . the grass looked so far away . . . she was too afraid!

CRASH!

Posey landed in a heap with her bike on top of her.

She started to cry.

"I hate riding bikes," she wailed. "It's too hard!"

Her mom ran out of the house.

"Calm down. You're all right,"

she said. She lifted off the bike. "Let me see."

She felt Posey's arms and legs. She checked for scrapes. "No harm done," she said.

"There was harm! I was afraid!" Posey cried. She wiped her face with her hand.

Blood!

"I'm wounded!" she cried.

"That's because of this." Her mom picked up something from the grass. "You lost your tooth."

Posey's tears stopped like

magic. She felt in her mouth with her tongue.

She had a space!

"You knocked it out when you fell." Her mom helped Posey stand up. "Let's go and wash your face."

Posey smiled her biggest smile in the bathroom mirror. She poked her tongue through her space.

She could hardly wait to show Grace and Ava and Nikki!

But she never wanted to ride that bike again.

CHAPTER
SIX

"I MISS MY MOMMY"

The tooth fairy left a crisp new dollar under Posey's pillow.

"Look," she said when her mom came into her room the next morning.

"Lucky you." Her mom sat on her bed. "Guess who called last night after you went to sleep?"

"Who?"

"Nikki's mom. Nikki invited you and Grace and Ava to a sleepover tonight."

"Can I go?" said Posey.

"If you want to. All you have to bring is your sleeping bag," said her mom.

Posey got her sleeping bag out of the closet. She packed her suitcase. She asked her mom, "Is it time yet?" about a million times.

Her mom drove her to Nikki's after lunch.

Her friends spotted Posey's space right away.

"Did it hurt?" Ava asked.

"I didn't even feel it." Posey told them about her bike crash.

"I don't want to take off my training wheels," said Nikki.

"One time, my daddy had to get stitches because he fell on his bike," Ava said.

They went outside and took turns jumping on Nikki's trampoline.

"You know what's impossible?" Posey yelled as she jumped. "It's impossible to jump so high, you touch the moon!"

They ate pizza for dinner. Then they watched a movie. After, they went up to Nikki's room to get ready for bed.

"Something's wrong with Ava," Grace said.

Ava was huddled on Nikki's bed.

She was crying.

"I miss my mommy," she said.

Posey and Grace and Nikki sat beside her.

Posey patted Ava's face. "You will see your mommy tomorrow," she said.

"I want to see her now," Ava cried.

"You better tell your mom," Grace told Nikki.

Ava's mom came and picked her up.

Posey and Nikki and Grace were very quiet after she left.

"Ava will be happy as soon as she gets home," Nikki's mom told them. "Some children aren't ready for sleepovers yet."

"When will Ava be ready?" Posey asked.

"When she feels it inside," said Nikki's mom.

She made them popcorn. Then it was time for bed.

Nikki's room was dark. Posey missed the streetlight outside her own bedroom window.

She missed her mom a little, too.

She put out her hand and touched Grace's sleeping bag. It was right next to hers.

She felt her tooth space with her tongue.

She would see her mom tomorrow.

CHAPTER SEVEN

GRAMPS IS BACK

Gramps's truck was in the drive-way when Posey and her mom got home the next day.

"Where's Mrs. Romero?" her mom asked.

"She's taking the train back," said Gramps.

Posey ran over and hugged him. "I thought you weren't coming home until the weekend," she said.

"And miss the chance of doing something special with my number one granddaughter?" said Gramps.

"Special like what?"

"How about looking for frogs' eggs in the pond again?"

"I want to!" Posey shouted.

Gramps lived in the country. Last spring, he and Posey found frogs' eggs and put them in a plastic jar. Posey watched them for weeks.

She saw the tiny black dot inside each egg grow into a squiggle. Then the squiggles started to move.

When the polliwogs hatched, she and Gramps put them back in the pond.

"What do you say we bring your bike along?" said Gramps.

Posey shook her head. "I don't want to ride it today."

"We'll bring it in case you change your mind," Gramps said.

"Okay. But only if I want to," said Posey.

"You're the boss," Gramps said.

"Wait just a minute!" Posey ran up to her room. She put on her tutu and stood in front of her mirror.

Princess Posey was brave.

She would get on that bike again.

Even if she was afraid, she would.

She would at least give it a try.

CHAPTER
EIGHT

RIDING LIKE
THE WIND

They found the net and jar in Gramps's garage. He put them in a plastic bag.

Then he took Posey's bike out of his truck.

"What do you say?" He patted the seat. "I'll hold on to you."

Posey had a feeling inside. Maybe she could do it.

"You better not let go," she warned.

"I won't," said Gramps.

Posey got on her bike. She gripped the handlebars hard.

"Ready?" Gramps asked.

"Ready."

Posey pushed down on the pedals. The bike started to go.

"Don't let go of me," she said.

"I'm right here," said Gramps.

The bike felt steady with Gramps holding on. Posey pedaled faster.

"Don't let go!" she called.

"I'm right behind you."

The road was straight and clear. Fields of tall grass were on both sides. Birds flew up when Posey rode past.

A squirrel dashed across the road ahead of her.

"You're doing great!" Gramps called.

The pedals went around and around. The tassels on the handlebars fluttered in the breeze.

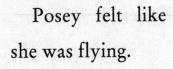

Posey felt like she was flying.

She felt like she could do anything.

She felt . . . exhilarated!

When she came to a path, she rolled to a stop and put her feet down.

"Is this where we turn?" she asked. She turned around.

She was on her own.

Gramps was far behind. He was jogging to catch up.

"Why did you let go of me?" Posey shouted.

Gramps caught up to her. "Let go of you? You took off on me!" He panted.

"What if I fell?" Posey yelled.

"Not you," said Gramps. "You were going like the wind."

Posey looked back. She rode all that way by herself.

"It was so easy," she said.

"Let's go find those eggs, speedy."

Posey spotted a clump of eggs under a log in the pond. Gramps scooped them up with the net and put them in the plastic jar.

They started back to his house.

Posey hopped on her bike.

"You need me to hold on to you again?" Gramps asked.

"I can do it." Posey started to pedal. "Try to keep up with me this time, slowpoke."

She rode like the wind all the way.

CHAPTER
NINE

A CRAZY, LAZY VACATION

The next morning, Posey rode up and down her driveway. She wanted Tyler and Nick to come out.

They finally did.

"Look at my new bike,"
Posey said.

They got their bikes out of their garage and came over to her.

"Pretty cool," said Tyler.

"Can you do a wheelie yet?" Nick asked.

"What's a wheelie?" said Posey.

"It's this." Nick rode a few feet. Then he jerked up on his handlebars. His front tire lifted into the air before it bounced back on the driveway.

"I can't do that," Posey said.

"Too bad." Nick and Tyler headed for the street.

"I can do it when I'm in second grade!" Posey shouted.

❀ ❀ ❀

On Saturday morning, Posey practiced turning. It was the only time her bike got shaky.

Her mom came outside with Danny. He climbed into his sand-box and started to dig.

Woof! Woof!

Posey saw Mrs. Romero walking Hero on the sidewalk.

"I want to show Mrs. Romero my bike," she said.

"Go ahead," said her mom.

Posey rode down her driveway and stopped at the end.

"I got a new bike!" she called.

"So I see." Mrs. Romero and Hero came up to her. "And you already know how to ride it."

Hero's tail went *whap! whap! whap!* against Posey's leg.

"It's so easy," Posey said. "Gramps couldn't even keep up with me."

"You lost a tooth, too!" Mrs. Romero cried.

"It fell out when I had my bike crash."

"A bike crash! What else happened while I was gone?"

Posey told her. She showed Mrs. Romero what the delivery man looked like.

"Zombies, a lost tooth, your first sleepover, and a bike crash . . ." Mrs. Romero laughed. "Your mom told me you were having a lazy vacation. It sounds more like a crazy one to me."

"It was a crazy, lazy vacation," said Posey.

CHAPTER
TEN

"YOU KNOW WHAT'S IMPOSSIBLE?"

Everyone wrote their stories in class on Monday morning. They shared them in the afternoon.

Luca wrote about his sister throwing up on a roller coaster ride.

Henry's story was about how he broke his arm by falling off their porch. He had a cast up to his elbow.

In Rashmi's story, she and her *nani* went to the top of the Empire State Building. "We were up so high. The pigeons were flying below us," she read.

Finally, it was Posey's turn.

"I crashed on my new bike and lost a tooth," Posey read. She opened her mouth wide so they could all see.

"My mom had a blue face," she

went on. "It scared the delivery man so much. He looked like this." Posey did her zombie imitation.

Everyone laughed.

Miss Lee collected the stories when they finished reading.

"Your stories were filled with interesting details," she said. "Best of all, I learned something. You know what's impossible?"

"What?" the class asked.

"It's impossible for a first-grader to have a boring vacation."

Watch for the next **PRINCESS POSEY** book!

PRINCESS POSEY
and the
FIRST GRADE PLAY

Posey wants to be the Queen Bee in the class play more than anything. When another girl gets the part, Posey is so upset! She does something that makes her feel better, but very soon realizes it was a terrible idea. Princess Posey and her tutu end up facing the toughest problem she has ever had to fix.